Debi Gregory's brilliant new children's book is a tale of five friendly young Elements who live deep in the forest.

With the simple but gorgeous line drawings (ideal for young hands to colour in!), we're introduced to Menme, the spirit imp; Tanwen, the fire sprite; Gwynt, the air imp; Dylan, the water sprite; and the earthy Celyn. Each has a distinct personality which is brilliantly captured in the artwork, and is a great way to help young children identify with feelings, both experienced by themselves and also how to recognise them in others.

The young Elemenpals encourage us to take a journey with them to visit the forces of Nature, and so we meet Mother Earth, Brother Sun, Sister Moon, Brother Oak and Sister River, with clear and easy to understand descriptions of their qualities and their nurturing powers. For very young children, it's a fantastic way for them to begin to understand what they can see around them, while also imagining them with friendly faces and personalities.

As the Elemenpals share their favourite things – both watching children play and engaging in activities that young readers will identify with – we're reminded of their distinctive characters and qualities, and how they fit in with Mother Earth and her fauna and flora.

This really is a beautifully illustrated and thoughtfully written book that is a great way for Pagan parents to introduce children to the wonders of Nature, while encouraging them to nurture and value the world around them.

An essential addition to every parent's bookshelf.

Candia McKormack, Singer/songwriter with Inkubus Sukkubus and deputy editor of Cotswold Life magazine

Quality books for Pagan children or children growing up in Pagan families are a little thin on the ground, especially when it comes to early readers. This imaginative and adorable creation fills that gap beautifully, with a gang of elemental beings who spark the desire to learn about the world and nature. I showed this book to both my nine-year-old and my one-year-old, and they both loved it. The nine-year-old related to the emotions displayed by the Elemenpals, and was immediately excited to know what further adventures they would be embarking on. My one-year-old found it soothing and was very interested in the pictures; it was a lovely way for us to bond together. This beautifully illustrated and engagingly written book is for any parent who wants to gently introduce the ideas of the elements, nature, reverence for our planet and even healthy expression of emotions.

Mabh Savage, Pagan parent and author of *A Modern Celt: Seeking the Ancestors, Pagan Portals: Celtic Witchcraft*

Elemenpals is a wonderful introduction to the elements, written for Early Years children. Through the adventures of the Elemenpals, young children will be excited to discover the magic of living nature. A fantastic creation by Debi Gregory, great for families, and schools alike.

Mike Stygal, Former President and current Vice President of the Pagan Federation, former teacher and member of the Inter Faith Council UK

Elemenpals
Come to Play

Elemenpals
Come to Play

Debi Gregory
Adam Greenwood

MOON BOOKS

Winchester, UK
Washington, USA

JOHN HUNT PUBLISHING

First published by Moon Books, 2020
Moon Books is an imprint of John Hunt Publishing Ltd., No. 3 East Street, Alresford
Hampshire SO24 9EE, UK
office@jhpbooks.net
www.johnhuntpublishing.com
www.moon-books.net

For distributor details and how to order please visit the 'Ordering' section on our website.

Text copyright: Debi Gregory
Illustrations: Adam Greenwood 2019

ISBN: 978 1 78904 525 3
Library of Congress Control Number: 2019952638

A CIP catalogue record for this book is available from the British Library.

Design: Stuart Davies

UK: Printed and bound by CPI Group (UK) Ltd, Croydon, CR0 4YY
US: Printed and bound by Thomson-Shore, 7300 West Joy Road, Dexter, MI 48130

We operate a distinctive and ethical publishing philosophy in all areas of our business, from our global network of authors to production and worldwide distribution.

Deep in the forest of a far away land,
in a big tree live the Elemenpals.
They are the best of friends.

There is Menme, the Spirit Imp.
Menme is very stubborn and bossy.

Tanwen, the Fire Sprite.
Tanwen is mischievous and silly.

Next is Gwynt, the Air Imp.
Gwynt is bad tempered and moody.

This is Dylan, the Water Sprite.
Dylan is emotional but brave.

The last is Celyn, the Earth Imp.
Celyn is sensible and kind.

Mother Earth made them so they
could grow up into strong Elements.
One day they will help the bigger
Elements to take care of
Mother Earth and her children.

But before they can do that, they
need to learn all about the planet and
how to take care of it.
Would you like to come too?

This is Brother Sun.
He keeps us warm. He brings the
daylight. He helps our flowers and
trees to grow.

This is Sister Moon. She calms
the tide. She brings the night time.
She helps the owls to see at night.

This is Brother Oak.
He is the Prince of the Forest.
He makes a home for woodland
creatures.

This is Sister River.
She flows through the Earth.
She brings life to the
world around her.

The 'Pals love their lessons.
They cannot wait to be big Elements
so they can take care
of Mother Earth.

They love to watch her children
while they learn.

Menme's favourite thing is when people sing. Menme loves to hear the beautiful melodies and loves to dance.

Tanwen's favourite thing is watching
the children build their sandcastles
at the beach. Tanwen especially
loves the shells they use to decorate
their towers.

Gwynt's favourite thing is to watch
the leaves dance in the wind.
Gwynt loves the reds, oranges and
yellows of the Autumn leaves.

Dylan's favourite thing is to watch
the fishes swim and splash. Dylan
loves their colours as they shimmer
and gleam.

Celyn's favourite thing is to watch
the rabbits as they bounce around.
Celyn loves their twitchy
noses and fluffy tails.

The Elemenpals are tired.
They have had a busy day showing
you their favourite things.
Will you come back again
to play with them?

They are snuggled back
inside their tree.
They are dreaming of the adventures
you will have together.
Good night 'Pals.
Sweet dreams.

Other fun activities!

Reading to your children is one of the greatest gifts you can give them. Not only are you giving them your undivided attention, you're showing them that books are there for their pleasure. Reading to your child daily is recommended to strengthen their future reading skills

Here are some other, some seemingly unrelated, ways you can help your children in their literary adventures!

- Play rhyming games.
- Encourage looking at books, even just the pictures.
- Talk to them as much as you can.
- Encourage games that include the use of hand-eye coordination.
- Do puzzles together.
- Promote the use of toys that support fine motor skills.
- Play "Dominoes" and matching games to help to promote association skills.

Some tips for doing these things in nature -

- Collect sticks or leaves and match them by size or colour.
- Watch clouds together.
- Play I-Spy.
- Explore textures, sizes and sounds by collecting sticks, leaves, feathers etc.
- Teach names of flowers, trees and wildlife and try to rhyme them.
- Draw pictures of the things you see and do.

You could even make a scrapbook of your fun and encourage them to get as involved as possible, encourage them to think of it as theirs so they can open the scrapbook, touch the things inside, look at the pictures and photos etc.

With this book, children are encouraged to relate to each Pal however their instincts first tell them to. Colour, gender, sex, ability etc have all been left as neutrally described as possible, to allow your children to fit the characters into their own narrative, their own world, their own idea of what a protagonist looks like in the way that's best for them. With this in mind, we've left the illustrations unfinished, with the hope that your children will colour and decorate them themselves and play a part in their own imaginings of these stories! And we'd love you to show us some of the finished works! You can email them to elemenpals@gmail.com or pop over to our social media pages –

Facebook - https://www.facebook.com/TheElemenpals/
Twitter - @elemenpals
Instagram - @theelemenpals

Let's share the magic!

Learning to read is about much more than just reciting phonics and these few tips, as well as having fun and encouraging family time, promote many innate skills that will be essential in your children's education and life.

Communication, as well as being our primary source of socialising and expression, is also an often-untapped resource for play! Words, sounds, body language; these are all toys with which you and your child can explore emotions, understandings, risks, pleasures or even just, plain silliness! Show your children, while you're reading to them, that the cadence and micro-communications in your voice and body language can convey meanings that words alone can't account for.

A story is more than words on a page, a story is a gift of many shades, many variations and every time you read a story to your child, you're giving them a new gift with each page.

"... children are active agents in their own development."
Bateson, P. (2001) 'Where does our behaviour come from?', *Journal of Biosciences*, vol. 26, no. 5, pp. 561–70.

Other Moon Books you might enjoy…

Moon Books Gods & Goddesses Colouring Book
Rachel Patterson
978-1-78279-127-0 (Paperback) £9.99 $14.95

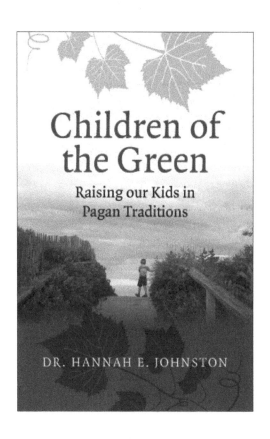

Children of the Green: Raising our Kids in Pagan Traditions
Hannah E. Johnston

978-1-78279-374-8 (Paperback)
978-1-78279-373-1 (e-book)

Let's Talk About Pagan Festivals
Siusaidh Ceanadach
978-1-78099-463-5 (Paperback)
978-1-78099-464-2 (e-book)

Let's Talk About Elements and The Pagan Wheel
Siusaidh Ceanadach
978-1-78099-561-8 (Paperback)
978-1-78099-562-5 (e-book)

Let's Talk About Rites of Passage, Deity and the Afterlife

Siusaidh Ceanadach

978-1-78099-945-6 (Paperback)

978-1-78099-946-3 (e-book)

**MOON
BOOKS**

PAGANISM & SHAMANISM

What is Paganism? A religion, a spirituality, an alternative belief system, nature worship? You can find support for all these definitions (and many more) in dictionaries, encyclopaedias, and text books of religion, but subscribe to any one and the truth will evade you. Above all Paganism is a creative pursuit, an encounter with reality, an exploration of meaning and an expression of the soul. Druids, Heathens, Wiccans and others, all contribute their insights and literary riches to the Pagan tradition. Moon Books invites you to begin or to deepen your own encounter, right here, right now.

If you have enjoyed this book, why not tell other readers by posting a review on your preferred book site.

Medicine for the Soul
The Complete Book of Shamanic Healing
Ross Heaven
All you will ever need to know about shamanic healing and how to
become your own shaman...
Paperback: 978-1-78099-419-2 ebook: 978-1-78099-420-8

Shaman Pathways – The Druid Shaman
Exploring the Celtic Otherworld
Danu Forest
A practical guide to Celtic shamanism with exercises and
techniques as well as traditional lore for exploring the Celtic
Otherworld.
Paperback: 978-1-78099-615-8 ebook: 978-1-78099-616-5

Traditional Witchcraft for the Woods and Forests
A Witch's Guide to the Woodland with Guided Meditations and
Pathworking
Mélusine Draco
A Witch's guide to walking alone in the woods, with guided
meditations and pathworking.
Paperback: 978-1-84694-803-9 ebook: 978-1-84694-804-6

Naming the Goddess
Trevor Greenfield
Naming the Goddess is written by over eighty adherents and
scholars of Goddess and Goddess Spirituality.
Paperback: 978-1-78279-476-9 ebook: 978-1-78279-475-2

Shapeshifting into Higher Consciousness
Heal and Transform Yourself and Our World with Ancient
Shamanic and Modern Methods
Llyn Roberts
Ancient and modern methods that you can use every day to
transform yourself and make a positive difference in the world.
Paperback: 978-1-84694-843-5 ebook: 978-1-84694-844-2

Readers of ebooks can buy or view any of these bestsellers by
clicking on the live link in the title. Most titles are published in
paperback and as an ebook. Paperbacks are available in traditional
bookshops. Both print and ebook formats are available online.

Find more titles and sign up to our readers' newsletter at
http://www.johnhuntpublishing.com/paganism
Follow us on Facebook at https://www.facebook.com/MoonBooks
and Twitter at https://twitter.com/MoonBooksJHP